# The Last Game

Written by
## James Hoffman

Illustrated by
## Diane Paterson

The ball park is full. It is the last
game of the year. All the players
from both teams are here.

The winner of the game will be
in first place. Both teams are ready
for what they will face.

The mothers and fathers come
for the fun. They cheer each batter
to hit a home run.

The game is well played and an even match. Many runs are saved by an amazing catch.

It is now the last inning. The game is a tie. The batter is up for one more try.

The ball is hit with a swing by Pat.
He is off and running at the
crack of the bat.

Shana runs back, close to the wall.
But as she looks up, she begins to fall.

The ball hits the wall and bounces toward Lee. He put out his glove, but it hits his knee.

The ball rolls to Pedro, who is covering first. He throws it to second, into the dirt.

Pat sees what happens and knows
at a glance, he can make it to third.
This is his chance.

The throw to third is missed by Jake.
Pat keeps running, right to home plate.

The ball takes a hop and skips
into the air. Haley turns quickly
to catch it up there.

Her foot hits the base which makes
her trip. Although she is falling,
she holds out her mitt.

She reaches out to tag him at the plate.
Pat is out. He slid in late.

But the game is not over when the score is a tie. The teams must keep playing, giving it one more try.